"Wow!"

D0832023

Thistle whispered to Axel. "Your potion really works."

"Yeah," Axel said. "I can't wait to see what happens next."

Everyone stared at Mrs. Pinch, Mrs. Pucker, and Mrs. Plum.

Their hair had grown long and wild.

Their teeth were sharp like fangs.

And their eyes glowed blood-red.

Before anyone could say a word, the three ladies stood up.

Then they began to howl…

MERCER MAYER'S
CRITTERS OF THE NIGHT ™

WEREWOLVES FOR LUNCH

Written by
Erica Farber and J. R. Sansevere

Bullseye Books
Random House 🏠 New York

A BULLSEYE BOOK PUBLISHED BY RANDOM HOUSE, INC.

Copyright © 1996 Big Tuna Trading Company, LLC.
CRITTERS OF THE NIGHT™ is a trademark of Big Tuna Trading Company, LLC.
All rights reserved under International and Pan-American Copyright
Conventions. Published in the United States by Random House, Inc., New York,
and simultaneously in Canada by Random House of Canada Limited, Toronto.

Library of Congress Cataloging-in-Publication Data
Mayer, Mercer.
Werewolves for lunch / written by Erica Farber and J. R. Sansevere.
    p. cm. — (Critters of the night)
"Bullseye books."
SUMMARY: Frankengator and Axel Howl get into big trouble when they
accidentally turn the three biggest gossips in Critter Falls into werewolves.
ISBN 0-679-87359-7
[1. Werewolves—Fiction.] I. Farber, Erica. II. Sansevere, J. R. III. Title.
IV. Series.
PZ7.F22275We   1996
[Fic]—dc20
95-6798
RL: 2.4
Manufactured in the United States of America   10 9 8 7 6 5 4 3 2 1

 A BIG TUNA TRADING COMPANY, LLC/J. R. SANSEVERE BOOK

CONTENTS

Wanda   Jack   Thistle   Axel

Bones

See

Snake

Capt. Short Bob   Dracul Duck   Wolf Mouse

Groad **Frankengator** **Moose Mummy**

Uncle Mole **Zombie Mombie** **Auntie Bell**

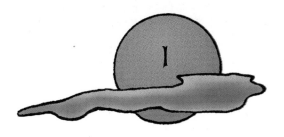

No Trespassing

"We're late," said Mrs. Pucker, glancing at the clock on the car dashboard.

Mrs. Pinch and Mrs. Pucker were on their way to Mrs. Plum's house. Every Tuesday night the three ladies played cards. They played Go Fish.

"I'd better take the shortcut by Old Howl Hall," said Mrs. Pinch.

Old Howl Hall was the oldest house in Critter Falls. It was also the biggest and the gloomiest. It was on the outskirts of town. There was a cemetery on one side and a swamp on the other.

No one had lived in Old Howl Hall for as long as anyone could remember.

"I wouldn't go near that place if I were you," said Mrs. Pucker. "It's downright creepy!"

"Ha!" said Mrs. Pinch. "I don't believe in any of that hocus-pocus."

"Well, I do," said Mrs. Pucker, puckering her lips. She always puckered her lips when she knew she was right.

"Nonsense," said Mrs. Pinch. She turned off the main road onto a dirt road. It was the shortcut that went past Old Howl Hall.

Suddenly, clouds moved across the sky. Lightning flashed. Thunder boomed.

"Where did this storm come from?" asked Mrs. Pinch, frowning.

The wind began to blow. Then it started to rain. It rained so hard that Mrs. Pinch could hardly see the road in front of her.

"The weather report didn't say anything about a storm!" said Mrs. Pinch.

But Mrs. Pucker was not listening to Mrs. Pinch. She was staring out the window in disbelief.

"That's funny," said Mrs. Pucker.

"What's funny?" asked Mrs. Pinch.

"Lights are on in Old Howl Hall!" said Mrs. Pucker.

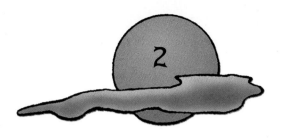

In a Pinch

"That's impossible," said Mrs. Pinch. "No one has lived in that house for years."

"Well, I see lights," said Mrs. Pucker. "I see them with my very own eyes."

"Well, your eyes must be playing tricks on you," said Mrs. Pinch.

"Oh, no, they're not," said Mrs. Pucker. "See for yourself."

Mrs. Pinch knew she shouldn't take her eyes off the road. But she just had to prove that Mrs. Pucker was wrong.

Mrs. Pinch turned her head and looked at Old Howl Hall. She couldn't believe it. Mrs. Pucker was right!

Lights were on in Old Howl Hall!

"Look out!" Mrs. Pucker yelled.

Mrs. Pinch turned her attention back to the road. Two big yellow headlights were heading straight for the car.

"You're in the wrong lane!" shouted Mrs. Pucker. She grabbed the wheel from Mrs. Pinch and yanked it to the right.

At the same time, Mrs. Pinch slammed on her brakes. The car skidded off the road and landed in a ditch, just as a big moving truck roared by.

"Now look what you've done!" said Mrs. Pinch.

"*You're* the one who drove off the road," said Mrs. Pucker.

"Yes, but *you* told me to look!" said Mrs. Pinch.

"Well, it was *your* idea to take the short-cut in the first place," said Mrs. Pucker.

Mrs. Pinch and Mrs. Pucker both got out of the car. Mrs. Pucker closed her door with a bang.

"Don't slam the door, Louise," said Mrs. Pinch.

Mrs. Pucker sniffed. "I didn't slam the door, Agnes. I simply shut it."

Mrs. Pinch looked around. "Now where in the world could that truck be going at this time of night?" she asked.

Just then the truck turned off the road. Mrs. Pinch and Mrs. Pucker watched as it drove up the long driveway that led to Old Howl Hall.

"Old Howl Hall!" said Mrs. Pinch. "How very odd."

"How shocking!" said Mrs. Pucker. "You know what they say about that house? A werewolf used to live there."

"That's ridiculous, Louise," said Mrs. Pinch. "There's no such thing as were-wolves!"

Mrs. Pinch and Mrs. Pucker stood in the rain and stared at the car. It was stuck in the mud.

"We'd better hurry to Beatrice Plum's

house," said Mrs. Pinch. "Maybe she knows something about what's happening at Old Howl Hall! You push, I'll steer."

"I think I should steer," said Mrs. Pucker. "And you push."

"It's my car!" shouted Mrs. Pinch. "*I* will steer and *you* will push. And that's final."

Mrs. Pinch got back in the car and stepped on the gas.

"Push!" she yelled out the window.

Mrs. Pucker pushed as hard as she could. The car didn't move.

"Push harder!" yelled Mrs. Pinch.

Mrs. Pucker pushed even harder. The car still wouldn't move.

"Come on, Louise," said Mrs. Pinch. "Push!"

Mrs. Pucker gave one mighty push as Mrs. Pinch stepped on the gas.

Suddenly, the car jumped backward.

"Get in, Louise!" yelled Mrs. Pinch.

Mrs. Pucker hopped into the car. Finally, Mrs. Pinch and Mrs. Pucker were on their way to Mrs. Plum's house again.

"What kind of critters would move into a place like Old Howl Hall?" asked Mrs. Pinch.

"*Creepy* critters," said Mrs. Pucker with a shudder. "Let's get out of here!"

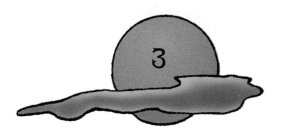

Home Sweet Howl

A flash of lightning lit up the sky around Old Howl Hall. The rain continued to pour.

"Marvelous weather for our first night in our new house," said Wanda Howl to her husband, Jack.

"Yes, perfect," said Jack.

The Howls stood in the front hall of their new home. There were cobwebs everywhere.

"A superb decorating job," said Wanda.

"Great-Grandpapa had won-
derful taste," said Jack. He
looked up at the stuffed animal
heads and old iron weapons
hanging on the walls.

Just then Groad walked into the room.

"I 'ave a question," said Groad.

Groad was the Howls' cook and butler.
He had been with the Howl family for gen-
erations. He came from a place he called
"gay Paree."

"Where is ze kee-chen?" asked Groad.

"You mean the kitchen," said Wanda.
"It's down the hall and to the right."

"Kee-chen . . . kitchen!" shouted Groad.
"You know exactly what I mean!"

He stormed out of the room.

"Groad seems a bit grumpy," said Wanda.

"It must be the move," said Jack.

Suddenly, there was a loud thud and the sound of breaking glass. The noise was coming from the drawing room.

"Sounds like the children are having fun," said Jack.

Wanda and Jack walked over and peeked into the drawing room.

Axel was kicking an iron ball and chain across the floor. His sister, Thistle, was trying to get it away from him.

"Isn't that sweet, dear?" said Wanda. "The children are playing soccer."

Axel kicked the ball. It went crashing into the fireplace. The painting above the mantel began to fall.

"Look out!" shouted Jack. "Great-Grandpapa is going to fall!"

Jack ran into the room. He caught the painting just as it fell.

"That was close," said Wanda.

Jack hung the painting up again.

Axel looked at the painting. "What was Great-Grandpapa Howl like?" he asked.

"He was a fine old critter," said Jack. "But I understand he wasn't exactly popular in Critter Falls."

"Why not?" asked Thistle.

"I believe the town critters were afraid of him," said Jack. "He had a beastly temper."

"Great-Grandpapa sure looks like one cool dude," said Axel.

"Yes," agreed Jack. "Great-Grandpapa traveled abroad a great deal, particularly in the desert. That was how he made his fortune. And then, of course, there were his inventions."

"Inventions?" said Axel. "What kind of inventions?"

"I don't know," said Jack. "He was a rather secretive chap."

"Now, children," said Wanda, "it's time to pick out your rooms."

"Okay," said Thistle. She ran to the stairs. "I want the room at the top of the tower."

"Make sure it doesn't have a lot of windows," called Wanda. "Too much sunshine isn't good for you."

"I'm going downstairs," said Axel. "I want to see if there's a dungeon."

"Good idea, son," said Jack. "A dungeon makes a fine bedroom for a growing boy."

Axel walked carefully down the stairs. They were steep and slippery. And it was very dark.

When he got to the bottom, he saw a big wooden door with a big bolt.

"Cool," said Axel. "This must be the dungeon."

Axel tugged on the bolt, trying to open the door. But no matter how hard he pulled, the door wouldn't open.

"Maybe I can break it down," said Axel.

He pounded on the door with his fist. *Bang. Bang.*

"Who's there?" someone growled from the other side.

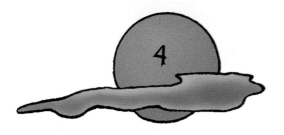

The Secret Potion

Axel's eyes opened wide. Who could that be? he wondered. Nobody lived in Old Howl Hall. He banged on the door again.

Bang. Bang.

"Who is it?" the same voice asked.

"Open the door!" said Axel.

"I'm not supposed to open the door to strangers," said the voice.

"I'm Axel Howl," said Axel.

"Well, why didn't you say so?" said the voice.

There was a squeaking sound as the bolt

was drawn. Then the door creaked open.

"Welcome to Old Howl Hall," said a large green critter with electrodes in his head. "I am Frankengator. I am the monster your great-grandpapa invented."

Axel walked into the room. It was big and dark and filled with all kinds of strange-looking equipment.

"Nice to meet you, Frankengator," said Axel, high-fiving the monster. "Is this the dungeon?"

"Yes, it is," said Frankengator. "And as you can see, it was also your great-grand-papa's lab. This is where I was born."

"Awesome!" said Axel, looking around the lab. His eyes lit up when he spotted a flask half-filled with a strange, glowing blue liquid.

"What's that?" asked Axel, pointing to the flask.

"That was the last thing your great-grandpapa was working on before he died," said Frankengator.

One big tear dripped down his cheek.

"Don't cry," said Axel. He reached up and patted the big green monster on the back.

"It's been very lonely here without him," said Frankengator. "I haven't had anyone to play with for years."

"I'll play with you," said Axel.

"Do you play checkers?" asked Frankengator.

"Yeah, but I'm not that good," said Axel. "My sister is a champion checker player."

"Goody," said Frankengator with a smile.

"I love to play checkers."

"What was Great-Grandpapa making?" Axel asked. He picked up the flask with the blue liquid.

"I believe it was a werewolf potion," said Frankengator. "The formula is in that big book on the table."

Frankengator pointed to a large leather book covered with dust.

Axel's eyes lit up. "A werewolf potion!" he said.

"Yes," said Frankengator. "But he never finished it."

"Well, tomorrow I'm going to finish making Great-Grandpapa's werewolf potion," said Axel. "And you can help me."

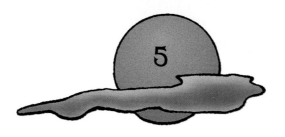

Table for Three

The next morning Mrs. Pinch, Mrs. Pucker, and Mrs. Plum were sitting at their favorite table at the Critter Falls Cafe. It was their favorite table because it was right next to the window.

They could see everything that was going on in Critter Falls.

Mrs. Pinch, Mrs. Pucker, and Mrs. Plum had their tea at the Critter Falls Cafe every morning at exactly nine o'clock.

"I think you should call, Louise," said Mrs. Pinch. "After all, you are the chairperson of the Welcome to Critter Falls Committee."

"That may be true, Agnes," said Mrs. Pucker. "But don't forget, *you* are the president of the PTA."

"Yes, but *your* husband is the mayor of Critter Falls," said Mrs. Pinch to Mrs. Pucker.

"Well, *your* husband is the chief of police," said Mrs. Pucker.

"Will you two stop!" shouted Mrs. Plum. "*I'll* call."

Mrs. Plum opened up her purse and pulled out a black mobile phone.

"My, my, Beatrice Plum. I didn't know you were so high-tech!" said Mrs. Pinch.

"Really!" agreed Mrs. Pucker.

"Well, you know what they say about the information superhighway," said Mrs. Plum. "If you don't get in the fast lane, you'll wind up as roadkill."

Mrs. Pinch and Mrs. Pucker exchanged glances. They both raised their eyebrows as Mrs. Plum punched some buttons on her phone.

"Do you have a new listing for Old Howl Hall?" said Mrs. Plum into her phone. "Thank you very much."

She punched some more buttons on her phone.

The phone at Old Howl Hall was in the hallway. Groad picked it up on the first ring.

"Allooooo, 'Owl residence," said Groad.

"Oh, excuse me," said Mrs. Plum. "I'm looking for the Howls."

"This ees the 'Owls," said Groad.

"I must have the wrong number, then," said Mrs. Plum. "I'm trying to reach Mrs. Howl."

"This ees the 'Owls," said Groad again.

"Oh, but I'm looking for the *Howls,* not the *Owls,*" said Mrs. Plum.

"This ees the 'Owls!" yelled Groad into the phone. "I will get Meesus 'Owl! Please 'old the fun!"

"Fun?" said Mrs. Plum. "What's a fun?"

"This ees a fun!" yelled Groad. "'Old on for Meesus 'Owl!"

Mrs. Plum held the phone away from her ear. "My, my!" she said. "Someone there has quite a temper."

"Who was it?" asked Mrs. Pinch.

"Must have been the butler," said Mrs. Plum. "He sounded foreign."

"How exotic!" said Mrs. Pucker.

Meanwhile, the Howls were having breakfast on the porch. They were looking out over the swamp. It was gray and very damp out. The fog had not lifted yet.

"Isn't the view lovely?" said Wanda.

"The only thing more lovely is you, Wanda," said Jack.

"Is Frankengator going to join us for breakfast?" Wanda asked Axel.

"No," said Axel. "He's not ready to come upstairs yet. He's still a little scared."

"Well, that's too bad," said Wanda. "I hope he comes up soon. We'll be gentle."

Just then Groad walked out onto the porch.

"Groad, these are the best mosquito pancakes you've ever made," said Wanda.

"And the slugs on toast are delicious," said Jack.

"Yep," said Axel. He took a big bite of slugs.

"And the swamp-dregs

tea is almost as good as my favorite, purple pickle juice," said Thistle.

"Fun for you, Madame," said Groad.

He handed the phone to Wanda.

"Hello," said Wanda into the receiver. ". . . How very thoughtful of you . . . Well, why don't you and your friends come over for lunch . . . Tomorrow at noon? . . . See you then."

Wanda hung up the phone.

She looked at Groad.

Groad looked at Wanda.

"Now, Groad, I know it's very short notice," said Wanda. "But three ladies from town want to welcome us to the neighborhood. Isn't that nice? So I invited them for lunch tomorrow."

"Grrrrr…" growled Groad.

"I was thinking you could make that wonderful Eye of Newt Soufflé and your special punch," said Wanda. "I'm sure the ladies would just love that."

"Tomorrow?!" exploded Groad. "I am an artiste. Not a fast-food cook. I can promise nothing. But, of course, I will do my best."

He stormed away.

"Can I be excused?" asked Axel. "Me and Frankengator have a lot of work to do in the lab. We're making a potion of Great-Grandpapa's."

"That's nice, dear," said Wanda. "Try not to be too good!"

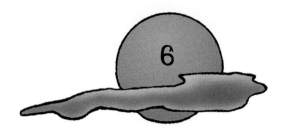

Mail-Order Mummy

Early the next morning, Axel couldn't stop yawning. He had been working on the werewolf potion all night long. And he was getting tired.

Axel looked at the formula in Great-Grandpapa's big leather book. All he needed were two more ingredients and the potion would be finished.

"Hey, Frankengator," said Axel. "We're almost done."

The only answer was a loud snoring sound. Axel turned around.

Frankengator was fast asleep. He was lying on his back on the floor with his legs up in the air.

Axel carefully measured out one tablespoon of mugwort. He sprinkled it into the potion. Then he scooped out a handful of soot and poured it on top.

The potion began to smoke as Axel finally fell asleep at the lab table.

A few minutes later, the front doorbell rang.

Groad ran down the hallway to answer it. He was still wearing his pajamas and nightcap.

"'Old your 'orses!" called Groad. "I'm coming."

Wanda came down the stairs. "Who could it be at this hour?" she asked.

Groad opened the door. He and Wanda looked outside.

There was nobody there. There was just a big wooden crate.

"I wonder what that could be," said Wanda.

She and Groad dragged the big wooden box inside.

"I'll get ze 'ammer," said Groad.

Groad went into the kitchen and got his toolbox from under the sink. Then he went back to the hallway. He began to pull the boards off the crate with his hammer.

He opened the crate. Inside was a large stone coffin.

"Oh, my!" said Wanda.

At that moment the lid of the coffin

popped open. A mummy wearing sunglasses sat up.

"Greetings! Greetings!" shouted the mummy. "I was going to send my favorite cousins a housewarming present. And then I thought to myself, 'Moosie, send yourself! What could be a better present?' I would have gotten here sooner if I hadn't gone third class. Traveling by mail isn't what it used to be."

Moose Mummy stood up and stretched. He looked around.

"I love what you've done to the house, Wanda," said Moose Mummy. "It's so sassy! It's so *you!*"

Just then Jack came down the stairs. Thistle was right behind him.

"Look who's here!" said Wanda. "It's Cousin Moose!"

Thistle ran over to Moose Mummy. She gave him a big hug.

"Cousin Moose, are you going to be in

any new movies?" she asked.

"Well, I'm up for three big parts," said Moose Mummy.

"Grrrrr..." said Groad. "Some movie star you are!"

"You're just jealous," said Moose Mummy. "Not everyone can be a big star like me."

"You are a movie star like I am the king of France!" said Groad. "You were only in one movie, and you didn't even 'ave any lines."

"Yes, but the director said I was a natural," said Moose Mummy.

"That's because you were playing a mummy, stupid!" yelled Groad. He stormed away.

"Cousin Moose," said Wanda quickly. "*We* thought you were marvelous in that film. Simply marvelous."

"Thank you, Wanda," said Moose Mummy. "I thought so, too."

"Hey, Moose," said Jack. "Let's throw the football around for old times' sake."

Jack and Moose Mummy were old football buddies. They had both played on the

Crittervania High School football team.

"Okay, Jack," said Moose Mummy with a big smile. "But no tricks."

"Tricks?" said Jack. "Not me."

Wanda followed Jack and Moose Mummy outside. She went into the garden.

"Oh, what a lovely garden," said Wanda to herself. "I've never seen so many different kinds of weeds."

She bent down and began to pull up weeds. She gathered the weeds into a big bunch. "These will make a lovely centerpiece for the table," she said.

On the other side of the garden, Jack and Moose Mummy were playing football.

"Okay, Moose, fake to the right, then go long for the bomb," said Jack.

Moose hiked the football to Jack. Moose ran to the right and stopped, then went long for the bomb.

Jack lit a small bomb, and threw it into the air.

Moose looked over his shoulder and caught it.

Boom! went the bomb.

The entire house shook from the huge explosion.

"Great catch!" said Jack.

Moose Mummy shook his finger at Jack. "You said no tricks," he said.

"Aw, Moose," said Jack. "I had to do it. For old times' sake."

Someone began to scream.

"Who's that?" wondered Moose Mummy.

"Oh, dear," said Wanda. "It sounds like Groad. I think we'd better go see what happened."

Wanda, Jack, and Moose Mummy all ran into the kitchen.

Groad was standing in front of the stove. He was wearing his apron and his chef's hat. He was jumping up and down and yelling things in French.

"What's wrong?" asked Wanda.

Groad didn't say anything. He just pointed to the oven. Inside were gobs and gobs of greenish gunk.

"What's that?" asked Wanda.

"Zat ees my Eye of Newt Soufflé!" shouted Groad. "Eet fell when zat big boom happened. And all of ze eyeballs popped out all over ze place."

Wanda looked around the kitchen.

Groad was right.
There were eyeballs all
over the floor and stuck
on the walls.

Axel and Thistle came into the kitchen.
"What made all that noise?" asked Thistle.

"Grrrrr . . ." said Groad.

"Groad's soufflé just went bye-bye," said
Moose Mummy.

"Shut up, you stupid moose!" yelled
Groad.

"Well, I finished my potion," said Axel.

He proudly put the flask filled with bub-
bling blue liquid on the counter right next
to Groad's special punch.

At that moment the doorbell rang.

"Oh, no!" said Wanda. "The ladies are
here already!"

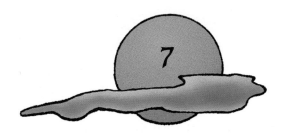

Three "P's" in a Pod

Mrs. Pinch, Mrs. Pucker, and Mrs. Plum stood on the front steps of Old Howl Hall.

Mrs. Pinch patted her head with one hand.

"Does my hair look all right?" she asked. "I had it done yesterday."

Mrs. Pucker and Mrs. Plum looked at Mrs. Pinch. Mrs. Pinch had just gotten a perm. Her hair was all curled up in a big lump on top of her head.

It looked terrible.

"It looks lovely, Agnes," Mrs. Pucker said.

Just then the door slowly swung open.

"Bonjour!" said Groad. "Or, should I say, 'ello."

Mrs. Pinch, Mrs. Pucker, and Mrs. Plum jumped back. They stared at Groad with wide eyes.

"Right this way, lay-deez," said Groad. "Mrs. 'Owl ees expecting you."

Mrs. Pinch, Mrs. Pucker, and Mrs. Plum followed Groad down the hallway.

As they looked around the house, their eyes opened wider and wider.

"Mrs. 'Owl will be right with you," said Groad. He left them in the drawing room.

Mrs. Pucker stared up at the portrait of Great-Grandpapa Howl over the fireplace. She nudged Mrs. Pinch.

"I told you a werewolf used to live here," said Mrs. Pucker, puckering her lips. She pointed to the portrait.

"Werewolf?" said Mrs. Plum in alarm.

"Ah, ladies," said Wanda, sweeping into the room. "It is a pleasure to meet you. I'm Wanda Howl."

"Agnes Pinch," said Mrs. Pinch, sticking out her hand. Then she pointed to Mrs. Plum. "This is Beatrice Plum."

"Pleased to meet you," said Mrs. Plum.

"And this is Louise Pucker," said Mrs. Pinch.

Mrs. Pucker didn't say anything. She didn't even turn around. She was still staring at the portrait of Great-Grandpapa Howl.

"A fine old gentleman, wasn't he?" said Wanda to Mrs. Pucker.

"Gentleman?" said Mrs. Pucker. "You mean werewolf, don't you?"

"Louise!" snapped Mrs. Pinch. "Control yourself!"

"True," said Wanda to Mrs. Pucker.

"Great-Grandpapa was a werewolf of the old school. A real pureblood. The last of a dying breed."

"Indeed, my dear," said Jack Howl, walking into the room. "And I understand he was quite a killer with the ladies, too."

Mrs. Pinch, Mrs. Pucker, and Mrs. Plum turned and stared in horror at Jack.

"Nice to meet you, ladies," said Jack. "Welcome to our home sweet home."

"As you can imagine, we're still getting used to the place," said Wanda. "It's so big and gloomy."

"Yes, it is rather creepy, isn't it?" said Mrs. Plum.

"I know," said Wanda. "Isn't it absolutely wonderful?"

Mrs. Plum, Mrs. Pinch, and Mrs. Pucker

looked at each other. They all raised their eyebrows in horror.

"Won't you have a seat?" said Wanda. "I believe it's time for some refreshments."

She picked up a mallet and hit a gong.

Bong. Bong.

The sound echoed through the house.

Mrs. Pinch, Mrs. Pucker, and Mrs. Plum all sank down onto the couch. Suddenly, something long and slimy slithered out of the couch and onto Mrs. Pinch's lap.

"Aaahhhh!" screamed Mrs. Pinch. She froze in terror.

Down the Hatch

"Meet Snake, our son Axel's favorite pet," said Jack Howl.

"What an original name," said Mrs. Plum nervously.

Snake curled himself around Mrs. Pinch's neck. He licked her face.

"He really likes you, Mrs. Pinch," said Wanda. "Now, Snake, stop being fresh. Leave Mrs. Pinch alone."

Snake uncoiled himself from around Mrs. Pinch's neck. He slithered across

the floor and out the door.

"Of all the—" began Mrs. Pucker.

Just then Moose Mummy walked into the room. Mrs. Pucker took one look at him and fell into a dead faint.

"Louise! Louise!" yelled Mrs. Pinch and Mrs. Plum. They both slapped her on the face to wake her up.

"Don't worry, ladies," said Jack. "I'm sure she'll come around in a minute."

"Greetings! Greetings!" said Moose Mummy. "Sorry about that. Sometimes I have an interesting effect on women. You have to get used to that sort of thing when you're in my line of work."

"And what line of work is that?" asked Mrs. Plum.

"The movies," said Moose Mummy. "I'm a movie star."

"Really," said Mrs. Plum. She stared at Moose Mummy.

"Weren't you in that movie *Mummy Dearest?*"

"Bingo!" said Moose Mummy with a big smile.

Mrs. Plum looked thrilled. "Can I have your autograph?" she asked.

"Beatrice, *really*," said Mrs. Pinch. "How horrible!"

"Oh, I don't mind," said Moose Mummy. He squeezed next to Mrs. Plum on the couch.

Mrs. Pucker's eyelids fluttered open.

"What did I tell you?" said Jack. "I knew she'd come around."

"Hello, hello," said Moose Mummy to Mrs. Pucker.

Mrs. Pucker took one look at Moose Mummy and fainted again.

"Wow!" said Moose Mummy. "She really has a thing for me."

"Where is that Groad?" Wanda said. She hit the gong again.

"You gonged, Madame?" said Groad, walking into the room.

"Yes, Groad," said Wanda. "I'd like you to bring our guests some refreshments."

"Yes, Madame," he said.

"If you'll excuse me for a minute," said Mrs. Pinch, "I need to use the ladies' room."

"Of course," said Wanda. "It's down the hall."

Mrs. Pinch walked out of the room. She went down the hall. She stopped in front of a door with a big lock on it.

At that moment the door opened. Frankengator came out. He looked at Mrs. Pinch. Mrs. Pinch looked at Frankengator. They both began to scream.

"Aaaaahhh!" Frankengator shouted. "It's a monster!"

"Aaaahhhh!" screamed Mrs. Pinch.

Frankengator turned and ran back down the basement stairs.

Wanda hurried into the hall. "Don't take

it personally," she said to Mrs. Pinch. "He's very shy. Especially around strangers."

Mrs. Pinch stared at Wanda. Her mouth opened and closed, but no words came out. Finally, she said, "I think I'll skip the ladies' room."

When they got back to the drawing room, Mrs. Pucker had come around again. And Groad was serving the refreshments.

"My, these are absolutely delicious," said Mrs. Pucker.

"Yes," agreed Mrs. Plum. She stuffed two more appetizers into her mouth. "What are they?"

"I call zem slugs in blankets," said Groad.

"Don't you mean pigs in blankets?" said Mrs. Pinch. She popped one into her mouth.

"No, I do not," said Groad. "Zey are not pigs. Zey are slugs. I dug zem out of ze mud myself."

Mrs. Pucker, Mrs. Pinch, and Mrs. Plum all began to choke.

"Don't worry, ladies," said Moose Mummy. He jumped off the couch. "What you need is some punch. It'll make those slugs slide right down your throat."

Mrs. Pucker, Mrs. Pinch, and Mrs. Plum all choked again.

Moose Mummy ran down the hall into the kitchen.

He grabbed the first thing he saw. Then he ran back to the living room.

"Moosie saves the day," said Moose Mummy.

He poured each of the ladies a glass of smoking blue punch.

Mrs. Pinch, Mrs. Pucker, and Mrs. Plum all took big gulps of the punch.

In a few seconds, they had drained their glasses.

Just then Axel and Thistle ran into the drawing room. "My potion's gone!" said Axel.

"Don't worry, dear," said Wanda. "You can always make more."

"You stupid moose!" yelled Groad. "You took ze wrong flask! You gave zese ladeez ze potion instead of my special punch."

"Well, the ladies really seemed to enjoy it," said Wanda.

"They drank it?" said Thistle.

"Uh-oh," said Axel. "Those ladies are in for a big surprise . . ."

My, What Big Fangs You Have!

"What exactly do you mean by 'a surprise?'" asked Mrs. Pinch. "I don't like surprises."

"Nor do I," said Mrs. Pucker. She puckered her lips.

"*I* like surprises," said Mrs. Plum.

Mrs. Pinch stared at Mrs. Plum.

"Why, Beatrice," she said. "What's wrong with your nails? They're so long and sharp. I thought you had them manicured yesterday."

"I did," said Mrs. Plum. She looked down at her hands. "My, my, these don't look like

my nails at all. They look like claws."

"And what is happening to your hair?" Mrs. Pucker asked Mrs. Pinch. "It's all a big mess."

"I *knew* you didn't like my hair," said Mrs. Pinch. "But you're behind the times, Louise Pucker. The hairdresser said curls are the latest thing."

Mrs. Pinch patted her head with her hand. But instead of short curly hair, she felt mounds and mounds of long curly hair.

"Oh, my goodness!" cried Mrs. Pinch. "My hair! My hair! What happened to my lovely short hair?"

"And what's wrong with your teeth, Louise?" Mrs. Plum asked Mrs. Pucker. "They are sticking out of your mouth—like fangs."

"What do you mean?" asked Mrs. Pucker. "I just went to the dentist last week. He said my teeth were perfect, as always."

Axel and Thistle stared at each other.

"Wow!" whispered Thistle. "Your potion really works."

"Yeah," agreed Axel. "These ladies are gonna be werewolves before they know it."

"What's happening to us?" shrieked Mrs. Pucker.

Everyone stared at Mrs. Pinch, Mrs. Pucker, and Mrs. Plum.

Their hair had suddenly grown long and wild.

Their teeth were all as long and sharp as fangs.

Their bodies were so big that their clothes were hanging off them in shreds.

And their feet were so large they had popped right out of their shoes.

On top of all that, their eyes glowed blood-red. Just like real live werewolves.

Before anyone could say another word, Mrs. Pinch, Mrs. Pucker, and Mrs. Plum stood up. They opened their mouths wide.

They began to howl. Just like real live werewolves.

"Awesome!" said Axel.

"Totally," said Thistle.

"Not bad for amateurs," said Jack. "Not bad at all."

Still howling, the three ladies ran across the room. They crashed through the picture window. And in a shower of broken glass, they were gone.

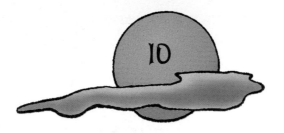

Smells Like Trouble

At the Critter Falls Police Station on the other side of town, Sergeant Pickle was just sitting down for a late afternoon snack.

Sergeant Pickle opened his lunchbox. Inside was a peanut butter and marshmallow sandwich. Sergeant Pickle picked up his sandwich. He licked his lips.

He was just about to take a bite when the phone on his desk rang.

"Critter Falls Police, Sergeant Pickle here," said Sergeant Pickle into the receiver.

"You saw a what? A *werewolf*?"

Just then another phone rang.

"Hold the line," said Sergeant Pickle. "I have another call."

Sergeant Pickle picked up the other phone.

"Critter Falls Police," said Sergeant Pickle.

He held the phone away from his ear. Someone was screaming. "You say a were-wolf is swimming in your pool?"

At that moment all the phones in the Critter Falls Police Station began to ring. Sergeant Pickle scratched his chin. He took a big bite of his peanut butter and marshmallow sandwich. He looked around at all the ringing phones.

In all his born days, he had never heard anything like it.

"I'd better call the chief," said Sergeant Pickle to himself.

Meanwhile, back at Old Howl Hall, Jack, Wanda, Axel, Thistle, Groad, and Moose Mummy ran downstairs to the dungeon.

"We need an antidote!" shouted Jack.

Frankengator had heard them coming. He hid under the lab table.

"Frankengator?" called Axel. "Where are you?"

"Under the table," said Frankengator. "And I'm not coming out."

"This is an emergency!" said Axel. "We need an antidote for the werewolf potion."

"A what?" asked Moose Mummy.

"You know, another potion to reverse the effects of the first potion," said Thistle.

"There isn't one," said Frankengator. He crawled out from under the table. "Great-Grandpapa hadn't invented one yet. See for yourself."

Axel looked through Great-Grandpapa's big leather book. No antidote!

"What are we going to do?" asked Wanda.

"Oh, those ladies are probably having the time of their lives," said Moose Mummy. "Why don't we just let them have fun?"

"Because they don't have the proper training!" said Wanda. "It takes centuries of study to become a true werewolf."

"That's right," said Jack. "Anyway, it's not in their blood."

"We have to turn those ladies back to their normal selves," said Wanda. "It's the only responsible thing to do."

"It says here that we have until midnight of the full moon to do it," said Axel. He looked up from Great-Grandpapa's leather book. "Or they'll be werewolves *forever!*"

"Tonight is the full moon," said Wanda. "We don't have much time."

"Then we'll have to do it the old way," said Jack. "I just hope I can find those ladies before it's too late."

"Jack, please be careful," said Wanda. "You don't want to end up like Great-Grandpapa . . ."

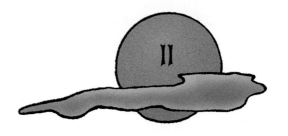

Full Moon Fever

The sun was setting over Critter Falls. Chief Lester Pinch of the Critter Falls Police was getting hungry.

He fired up the barbecue and cut up the lamb chops. Everything was ready except for one thing—his wife, Agnes Pinch, wasn't home yet.

Just then the phone rang.

"Chief Pinch," said Chief Pinch into the receiver. "Slow down, Sergeant. What in the world are you babbling about? Werewolves in Critter Falls? You're losing your marbles,

Sergeant . . . Now get a hold of yourself. And stop talking nonsense! There are no such things as werewolves!"

Chief Pinch slammed down the phone. Sometimes he wondered where Critter Falls would be without him.

Chief Pinch took the lamb chops outside. He put them down on the table next to the barbecue. Then he went back into the house to get Agnes's special barbecue sauce.

In a flash Mrs. Pinch, Mrs. Pucker, and Mrs. Plum jumped out of the bushes. They ran over to the table and began chomping on the lamb chops.

Mrs. Pinch loved lamb chops. But these lamb chops were the best she had ever tasted.

They were raw and bloody.

"Hey, you nasty critters, leave that food alone!" shouted Chief Pinch, running out of the house.

Mrs. Pinch looked up at her husband.

Chief Pinch stopped dead in his tracks.

"Grrrrr . . ." growled Mrs. Pinch, Mrs. Pucker, and Mrs. Plum.

"Agnes?" gasped Chief Pinch. "Louise? Beatrice?"

Mrs. Pinch, Mrs. Pucker, and Mrs. Plum bared their fangs and snarled.

Chief Pinch dropped the barbecue sauce. It splattered everywhere.

Before Chief Pinch could say another word, Mrs. Pinch, Mrs. Pucker, and Mrs. Plum ran off down the road. They were headed for Main Street.

"It was just a bunch of dogs, it was just a bunch of dogs," babbled Chief Pinch. Meanwhile, the ladies charged down Main Street. Doors and windows opened on every side. The critters of Critter Falls took one look at Mrs. Pinch, Mrs. Pucker, and Mrs. Plum. And they all began to scream.

Suddenly, a howling sound filled the air.

Mrs. Pinch, Mrs. Pucker, and Mrs. Plum froze in their tracks.

"AAAAHHHH-OOOOOHHHHH!" howled Mrs. Pinch.

"AAAAHHHH-OOOOOHHHHH!" howled Mrs. Pucker.

"AAAAHHHH-OOOOOHHHHH!" howled Mrs. Plum.

"AAAAHHHH-OOOOHHHH-OOOHHH!" howled something from the top of the hill on the edge of town. The full moon began to rise.

Mrs. Pinch, Mrs. Pucker, and Mrs. Plum dashed out of town. They ran as fast as they could toward the howling sound.

Back at Old Howl Hall, Axel and Thistle were listening to the howling, too.

"Hey," said Axel. "Listen to that wolf. It sounds like it's right outside the window."

Axel and Thistle ran over to the window. They looked outside.

There on top of a hill was a big silver wolf. The wolf opened its mouth wide. It let out another bloodcurdling howl.

Hocus-Pocus

"Awesome!" said Axel.

"Totally!" agreed Thistle.

Wanda walked into the dining room. "Okay, everyone, get ready," she said. "It's almost showtime."

Groad ran out of the kitchen with a tray heaped with raw meat. He set it on the dining room table.

"Nail clippers," said Wanda.

"Check," said Thistle, nodding.

"Silver key," said Wanda.

"Check," said Axel.

"Do you know your lines, Cousin Moose?" asked Wanda.

"I'm an actor, Wanda," said Moose Mummy. "I do this all the time."

Groad rolled his eyes.

Just then the doors of Old Howl Hall burst open. The big silver wolf charged inside. Mrs. Pinch, Mrs. Pucker, and Mrs. Plum charged in right behind it.

The wolf ran across the dining room and jumped out the window.

Mrs. Pinch, Mrs. Pucker, and Mrs. Plum stopped short as they spotted the raw meat. They jumped on top of the dining room table and began to stuff themselves.

"Action!" shouted Wanda.

Thistle went over to Mrs. Pinch and in an instant clipped off a tiny piece of her claw. Then she did the same to Mrs. Pucker and Mrs. Plum. The ladies were too busy eating to notice.

Axel tapped each lady on the top of the head with the large silver key.

All eyes turned to Moose Mummy. The mummy just stood there, frozen.

He couldn't say a word.

"Clip of nail, tap of key, Beatrice a were-wolf shall not be!" yelled Groad at the top of his lungs.

Suddenly, Beatrice Plum's fangs disappeared. So did her claws. Within seconds, she returned to her normal self.

"Clip of nail, tap of key, Louise a were-wolf shall not be!" shouted Groad. Then:

"Clip of nail, tap of key, Agnes a werewolf shall not be!"

Instantly, Mrs. Pucker and Mrs. Pinch were transformed back to their normal selves, too.

Mrs. Pinch turned to Mrs. Pucker. "Louise, what on earth are you doing on the table?" she asked.

"You mean, what are *you* doing on the table, Agnes?" replied Mrs. Pucker. "And what in the world did you do to your clothes? And what are you doing with all that garbage in your hair?" she asked.

Then she climbed off the table.

Mrs. Pinch carefully got off the table, too.

"Will you two stop it!" said Mrs. Plum. "Can't you see we're all a mess?"

"The last thing I remember is drinking that strange blue punch," said Mrs. Pinch.

"Me too!" said Mrs. Pucker, frowning. "Everything after that is a big blur."

"Well, whatever happened," said Mrs. Plum, "I had a lot of fun!"

"Fun!" said Mrs. Pinch. "You call that fun? Well, I think we've all had enough 'fun' for one day. Now come along, Louise. You too, Beatrice."

Mrs. Pucker and Mrs. Plum followed Mrs. Pinch out of Old Howl Hall. The three ladies got into Mrs. Pinch's car and drove away.